HE Bear SHE Bear

by Stan and Jan Berenstain

COLLINS

For Leo and Robin

Trademark of Random House, Inc., William Collins Sons & Co. Ltd., Authorised User

6 7 8 9 10

ISBN 0 00 171269 1 (paperback)
ISBN 0 00 171217 9 (hardback)

Copyright © 1974 by Stanley and Janice Berenstain
Illustrations Copyright © 1974 by Random House Inc.
A Bright and Early Book for Beginning Beginners
Published by arrangement with
Random House Inc., New York, New York
First published in Great Britain 1975

Printed in Great Britain by
William Collins Sons & Co Ltd, Glasgow

HE BEAR SHE BEAR

I see her.
She sees me.

We see that we
are he and she.

Every single
bear we see
is a he bear
or a she.

Every single
bear we see
has lots of things
to do and be.

I'm a father.
I'm a he.
A <u>father's</u> something
<u>you</u> could be.

I'm a mother.
I'm a she.
A <u>mother's</u> something
<u>you</u> could be.

Dad's a he.
Mum's a she.

Those are things
that we could be
just because
we're he and she.

But there are
other things to be.
Come on, He Bear,
follow me!

We could . . .

fix a clock,

paint a door,

build a house,

have a store.

Drive a
dump truck,

drive a crane,

bulldoze roads,

drive a train.

We fix clocks,
we paint doors,
we build houses,
we have stores.

We bulldoze roads,
we drive cranes,
we drive trucks,
we drive trains.

We can do all these things,
you see,
whether we are he or she.

We climb ladders
to fix the wires.

We climb ladders
to put out fires.

That's Officer Marguerite.
She tells us when
to cross the street.

You could . . .

Be a doctor—
make folks well.

Teach kids how
to add and spell.

Knit a sock,

sew a dress,

paint a picture—

what a mess!

You could . . .

Lead a band,
sing a song,
play a tuba,
beat a gong.

Play a banjo—
plink-a-plink.
You could even play
on a kitchen sink.

We have stores,
we fix clocks,
we are officers,
we knit socks.

We teach kids how
to add and spell,
we drive, we build,
we make folks well.

We climb ladders,
we sew dresses,
we make music,
we make messes.

We can do all these things,
you see,
whether we are he or she.

What will we do,
you and I?

I'll tell you what
I'm going to try . . .

I may build bridges,

I may climb poles,

I may race cars,

I may dig holes.

I could be a magician,

I could go on TV,

I could study the fish
who live in the sea.

I'll be a cowboy,

I'll go to the moon,

I'll feed a whale,

I'll train a baboon.

We'll fly a giant
jumbo jet.

We'll build the tallest building yet.

We will jump
on a trampoline.

We'll do tricks
that have never
been seen.

We'll tame
twelve tigers . . .

and twenty-six fleas.

We'll do a dance
on a flying trapeze.

We'll jump and dig
and build and fly. . . .
There's <u>nothing</u> that
we cannot try.

We can do all these things,
you see,
whether we are he OR she.

So <u>many</u> <u>things</u>
to be and do,
He Bear, She Bear,
me . . . and you.